This Book Belongs To:

DRAGONS AND HOT SAUCE
AND OTHER IMAGINATIONS

Written by Mike Moore
Illustrated by Andy Young

ISBN-13: 978-1505391398

ISBN-10: 1505391393

First Printing 2014

Contact Information: dragonsandhotsauce@gmail.com

Cover and interior illustrations by Andy Young

Book design by Jim Campbell, Campbell Arts

Printed in the United States of America

ACKNOWLEDGMENTS

Thank you to everyone who helped with and supported this book along the way - too numerous to name here, but so, SO appreciated!

DEDICATED TO:

To Lily, I hope these make you smile. Love, Dad.
— Mike

To my Daughters Audrey and Nora.
— Andy

RIBBONS

Little Lily Lambert loved
　　Big red ribbons in her hair
Every time she went outside
　　The kids would stop and stare
Lily said she didn't see
　　Why the others found it weird
That she loved those ribbons tied
　　In her bushy, yellow beard

BALLOON

I wished I was a big balloon
To float above the town
Now breezes blow me here and there
So I can watch the ground
I watch the trees and parks and lakes
In greens and blues and browns
But now I need a second wish
So I can get back down!

KITTIES

Kitties, kitties in the tree
Playing in the morning sun
Slink and scramble, pounce and leap
Watch the birds and jump and run

Sun is warm upon your fur
Wind is tick'ly on your nose
Leaves are whispery in your ear
Bark is rough between your toes

We're all glad you're having fun
Way up in your leafy tower
But now it's time to come back down
We've been waiting here for hours

DRAGONS AND HOT SAUCE

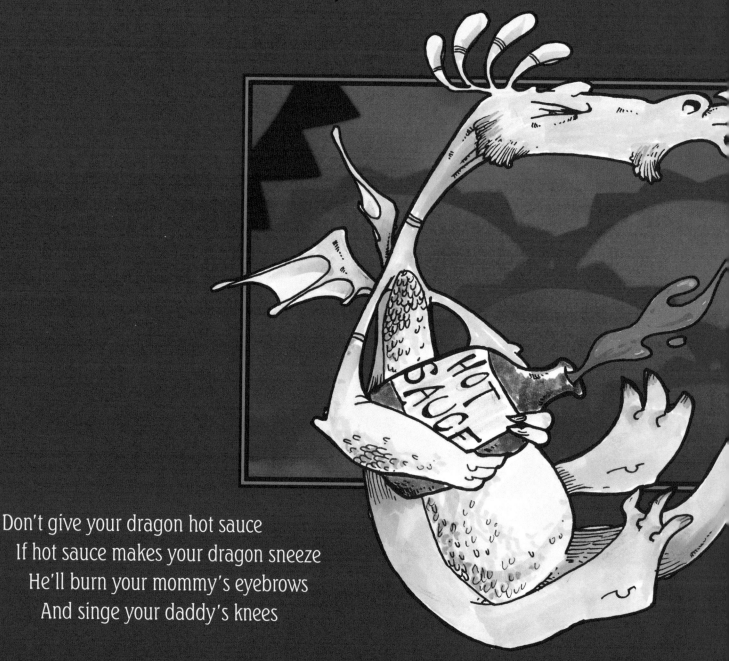

Don't give your dragon hot sauce
If hot sauce makes your dragon sneeze
He'll burn your mommy's eyebrows
And singe your daddy's knees

He'll make your toast too toasty
With every big "ah choo Choo CHOO!!!!"
And you'll be way too roasty
If he sneezes right at you

But if a dragon ate MY hot sauce
Do you know what I would do?
I would squeeze that sneezy dragon
And have myself a bar-b-que

AMAZING SiR RANDY

My name is Sir Randal Randolpho
That's "Amazing Sir Randy" to you
And no one has dared me a dare
That I haven't been able to do

I once chewed a whole pack of gum and
Blew bubbles as big as the moon
I've clambered up trees like a monkey
With Clive (he's the king of baboons)

I've juggled live sharks by the tail
I've held dancing lions upright
And now for my biggest stunt yet

I WILL EAT ALL MY VEGGIES TONIGHT!

DETECTIVE

My name is detective Pierre
My partner is Bunny St. Clair
A thief ate my lunch
And I've got a hunch
The culprit's a hairy brown hare

SUZIE SNOOZEALOT

They called her Suzie Snoozealot
She spent whole months asleep
A winter came; a winter went
She never made a peep
They finally called a doctor out
Who gave them all a scare
He said, "Suzie is actually
a hibernating bear!"

DRAWINGS

If you drew pictures
And they'd come to life
What do you think
you'd make?

Would you draw monsters?
Make believe lands?
The world's biggest milkshake?
It's simple for me
I don't have to think
I know just what I'd do

I would get paper
And get lots of pens
Then make drawings of you

Moon

I ride my bike
out on the moon
And ramp off all
the soft white dunes
There is no air,
there's just starlight
And me, afloat,
in arcing flight
With grace, with style,
I show my worth
And wow the folks
on planet Earth

GIRAFFE

I once knew a lovely giraffe
Who hated to take a bath
With his head way up there
Just washing his hair
Took at least a seven man staff

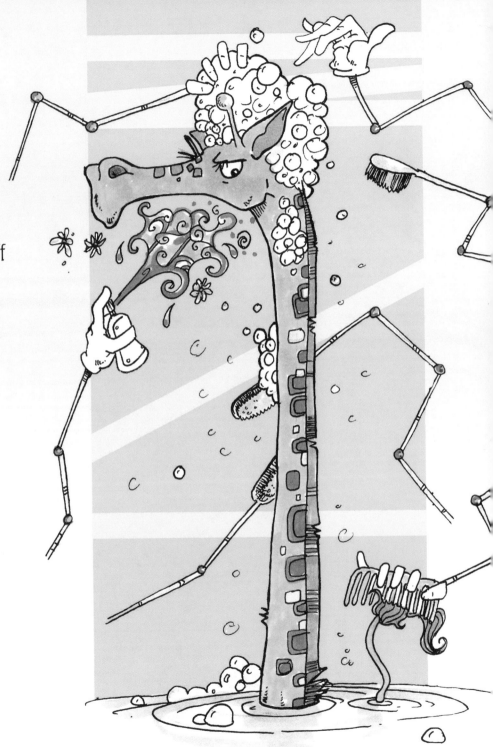

BEDTIME

I'm the beast under your bed
I know you think I'm scary
Parts of me have shiny scales
And other parts are hairy

But I have a special job
I guard you in your bed
And take all of the bad dreams
From your sleeping head

My scales light the long dark night
While I watch over you
So the only dreams you dream
Are good and kind and true

When the morning comes I slink
Beneath the bed again
And dream my own sweet dreams of you
You, my dearest friend

SNOWMAN

Steve had to eat ice cream
Every meal of the day
Because if he didn't
He was sure to melt away

You see, Steve was a snowman
Who didn't have a care
Until he took a hairdryer
And tried to dry his hair

IMAGINATION

They told me, "Go sit still"
So I sailed the seven seas
In my fearsome pirate ship
With my mates (and all their fleas)

They told me to be quiet
So I belted out a tune
With my friends, the mermaids
From the Lost Lagoon

They told me I was odd
My clothes were not quite right
Then I donned my super suit
And flew into the night

They told me not to dream
But there's so much I can be
And with my imagination
I'll do anything I please

PILOT

Ernie was an Emu
With short and stubby wings
But he wished that he could fly
More than anything

He'd take a running start
And he'd jump up and down
Then he'd flap and flap those wings
But never leave the ground

So he used his head
And hatched a bird-brained scheme;
He would find another way
To reach his flying dream

He'd work really hard
And study night and day
So once he passed his pilot's test
He could fly away

A DOG'S HAIKU

Warm sun, fur, and grass
Let's roll and wiggle around
Uh-oh ... mud ... bathtime!

BiGFooT

I hope we don't find Bigfoot
We're just not ready yet
We don't even know
If he should go
To the doctor …
Or the vet

TICKLEMONSTER

Beware the Ticklemonster, friend
He might sneak up on you
And he'll start to tickle 'cause
That's what he's built to do!

To tickle you, he has 10 hands
With extra finger joints
He keeps a scoreboard in his room
To track his tickle points

But don't be scared, he's not mean
He's actually quite meek
You see, the Ticklemonster has
Some big ole' ticklish feet!

COOTIES

Sammy liked Susie and Susie liked Sammy
But cooties stood in their way
So they both went and got cooties shots
And then ran off to play

They had so much fun! They'd laugh and they'd giggle
They'd tickle, they'd scream, they'd shout
And then everyone was happy except
The cooties - who felt left out

AWESOME SHOP

My mom works at The Awesome Shop
They make your dreams come true
If you can dream up anything
They'll make it just for you

She doesn't drive a car to work
She rides a grizzly bear
And everyone gets jetpacks!
They never use the stairs

They have a vault of everything
That's known or thought or said
And when you're really, REALLY stuck
They beam it to your head

So when you make the 3-point shot
Or when you ace your test
Be sure to say thanks to my mom
For making you the best

WEDDING

I saw a picture of a princess
On her wedding day
She wore a simple dress of white
Her prince, a suit of gray

They looked so young and perfect
At their wedding by the lake
With flowers, friends and family and
A layered wedding cake

I asked my mother who they were
I thought that I should know
She smiled, "That's your parents
From a long, long time ago!"

I didn't understand at first
And then thought suddenly
That if they were those people
Were they once as young as me?

RUBBER DUCK

I know you don't like bathtime
I'm even more unlucky
You're a smelly human
I'm a hydrophobic ducky

CRAB WALK

You know what I think would be totally fab?
To walk around sideways, just like a crab

I'd care so much less about how to get to
And care so much more about where I went through

I'd get a good look at the places I passed
And maybe walk slower, instead of so fast

I'd tell you about all the buildings and trees
The blossoming flowers and bright, buzzy bees

And how it is not about getting somewhere
Instead it's the places between here and there

CoME QUICK

Mom, Mom come quick
Up in the sky
The sun sent a cloud
I think it's a spy!

Mom, Mom come quick
Up in the tree
That silly old bird
Is staring at me!

Mom, Mom come quick
Up on the wall
A spider is dangling
I'm worried he'll fall!

Mom, Mom come quick
There are things bright and new
And Mom I just wanted
To share them with you!

PRINCESS POLLY

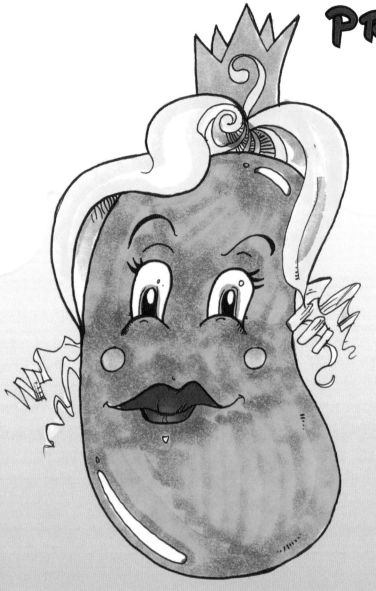

Princess Polly Pollyanne
Was the fairest in the land
Men would come from all around
Set to try and win her hand

Smiling lips were cherry red
Flashing eyes a lime-y green
Hair to frame her perfect face
Had a lemon yellow sheen

Known as gentle, kind and fair
Just the sweetest that they'd seen
Part of it was prob'ly that
Polly was a jellybean

UNICORN

I tried to go camping
And roast a hot dog
But couldn't find a stick
So I went and imagined
A brand new friend
He's a unicorn (named Mick)

He doesn't have thumbs
So he can't hold a lot
But he's got a fireproof horn
He'll roast you 3 hot dogs
And 7 marshmallows
And even an ear of corn

He's easy to talk to
And fun in a group
He juggles and does magic tricks!
I'm really quite proud
Of my made up friend
The unicorn (named Mick)

Pool PARTY

I threw my friends a pool party
We were having fun
Hanging out and laughing
Playing in the sun

That's when Sammy squirted Susie
Susie tried to go dunk Billy
Someone called out, "WATER FIGHT!"
Things had gotten silly

People grabbed their water guns
Someone grabbed the hose
Someone else filled up balloons
And started throwing those

Then we realized our mistake
We'd forgotten one big rule:

Pool parties always end
When there's no water in the pool

MEALS

My dinosaur will not eat lunch
Until he's finished up with brunch
Brunch comes after morning snack
Which follows breakfast (back to back)

After lunch, he eats three times
Before we hear the dinner chimes
He'll finish with a few desserts
And then complain his stomach hurts!!

SWIM LESSONS

I will learn to swim
So I can swim with sharks
Explore the hidden places
Of the ocean deep and dark

I'll search out sunken treasure
And long lost pirate's booty
It's my dream, my life, my calling
I might even say, my duty

I know that I will be the best
Swimmer in this town
But first, could you instruct me, please
How do I not drown?

THE TALE OF SIR FLUFFYTAIL

My names are Sir Sharpfang,
Quickpounce, and Fiercenail
My humans just call me
Monsieur Fluffytail
My grace is unmatched
My speed is divine
You **could** say that I
Am a gifted feline
They've written whole songs on
The sheen of my fur
(Or maybe not yet — They will soon, I'm sure)
My senses are keen
I can hear a pin drop
(Or I thought I did once — It was only a mop)
I'm silent and stealthy
I don't make a peep
(Except in the mornings when I'm still half asleep)
I'm king of the jungle
Or at least of this house
(I just have to work on my fear of this mouse!)

RAFTERS

I spent some time in the rafters
And didn't make a sound
It's amazing what you learn
When you take a look around
By seeing where they're looking
You can tell what someone thinks
Do they like who they're with
Or think that person stinks?

Are they happy with their friends
Or are they really bored?
Do they feel valued or
Do they feel ignored?
Or did they find the person
That's closer than a brother
While they sometimes glance away
They come back to each other

NEW BABY

"We're going to have a new baby"
My Mommy just told me
But I think I like it how it is
My Mommy and Daddy and me
I'll have to clean up my room more
And probably share all my toys
They even said that it might be
An icky, grody BOY

I'll have to teach him how to swim
And sing and play and run
Well hold on now … could it be?
This brother might be … fun?!?
We're going to have a new baby
He'll be my new family
And I'm going to be the biggest, bestest
Sister I can be

ANOTHER WORLD

I learned that there's another world
Hidden beneath ours
For dessert they eat their veggies
Dinner's candy bars
I hear their puppy dogs meow
I'm told their cats all bark
The moon is always bright as day
The sun just makes things dark
And everyone is born quite old
And then turn into babies
And when someone promises
They always promise, "maybes"
Still, there is at least one thing
That's just as true as true
When they really, REALLY care
They all say, "I love you"

SPACE CHICKEN

If I had a rocketship
I'd travel to the star
Where my friend Space Chicken
Would play me his guitar
He would pluck and strum the strings
While clucking out a song
It would only have one lyric
So I could sing along

"Cluck cluck" we would resonate
Then "cluck cluck" once again
Space Chicken would harmonate
About some pretty hen

As the night is ending
I'd go home and off to bed
With the chicken's spacey song
Still playing in my head

SUPERDOG

We tried to teach our dog new tricks
He didn't understand
So we tried to make him smart
And things got out of hand

We made his brain much bigger
But were so surprised to find
Instead of learning "sit" he was
An evil mastermind!

Saying he's a bad, bad dog
Doesn't seem quite right
When he's had the mailman in
The basement since last night

He wants to rule the world
We'll put a stop to that!
We've got plans to supercharge
The next-door neighbor's cat

MUMMY

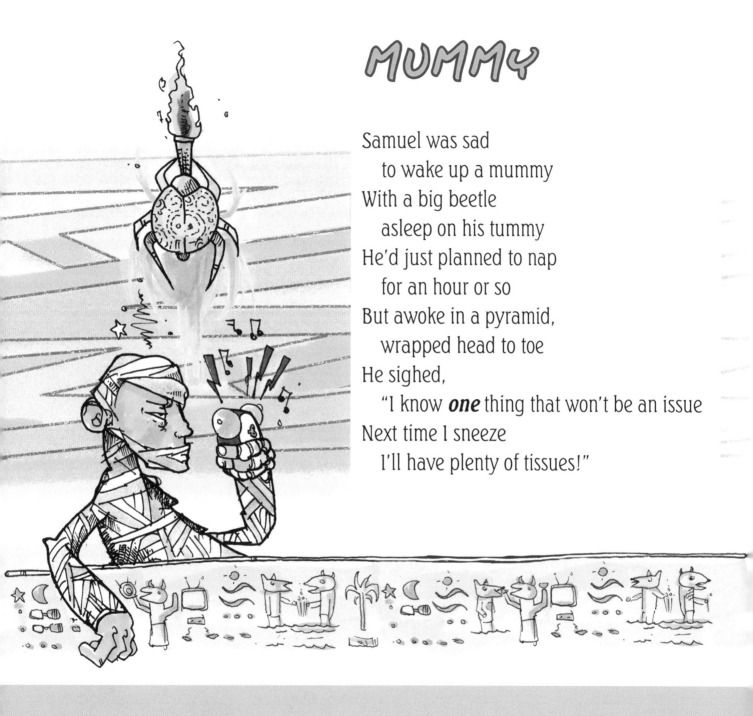

Samuel was sad
   to wake up a mummy
With a big beetle
   asleep on his tummy
He'd just planned to nap
   for an hour or so
But awoke in a pyramid,
   wrapped head to toe
He sighed,
   "I know **one** thing that won't be an issue
Next time I sneeze
   I'll have plenty of tissues!"

GiANT

If you want to take a bath
You prob'ly think it's cake
Unless you are a giant
And need a giant lake

When you're mighty tired
And need to go to bed
You need a giant mountain range
To rest your giant head

And right before you fall asleep
You need a giant hug

'Cause every single giant
No matter how big
No matter how tall
The scary, mean, fierce ones
Or giant goofballs

Every giant likes to be
Tucked in all safe and snug

Titles are set in Andy Young, Medium, 42 pt

Lettering design: Andy Young,

Font design: Jim Campbell, Campbell Arts

•

Text is set in Seagull, 16 pt, condensed

Designers: Adrian Williams and Bob McGrath

Publisher: Bitstream, Inc.

'Seagull' is a trademark of Ingrama S.A.